BUGS BUNNY

SEE BUGS BUNNY'S
MAGIC SHOW

Flip the pages rapidly and watch the
pictures in upper right-hand corner as
the characters seem to come alive!

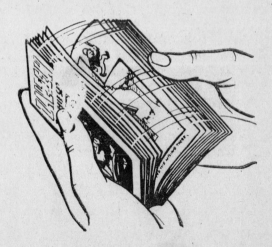

BUGS BUNNY

and

KLONDIKE GOLD

Authorized Edition

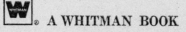 ® A WHITMAN BOOK

Western Publishing Company, Inc.

Racine, Wisconsin

CONTENTS

"What's Cooking, Porky?"

CHAPTER 1

FROSTY FRED

Bugs Bunny elbowed his way through the crowd that was packed five deep along the curb and spied his pal, Porky Pig.

"What's cooking, Porky?" he asked. "What's all the mob gathered for?"

Porky was so excited that he stuttered as he replied. "Th-they're waiting for Frosty Fred! He's the richest gold miner in the whole world!"

Bugs looked again at the eager mob and scratched one of his fuzzy ears, puzzled. "So what?" he questioned. "There are plenty of rich guys in the world! What's he got —two heads or something?"

"Gosh, no!" Porky answered impatiently. "But he gives away real gold pieces once a year, and he's due any minute! I'm here to get mine!"

Bugs twitched his ears and

"We're Waiting for Frosty Fred!"

stretched his skinny neck for a look up the street. "In that case," he announced, "I'll hang around and latch on to a couple hunks of the shiny stuff myself. I can always use a little extra carrot dough!"

The crowd kept edging forward until Bugs and Porky were forced nearly out into the street. "So old Frosty Fred tosses gold away!" Bugs said wonderingly. "He must be loaded!"

"He is!" Porky agreed. "They say he got it all up in Alaska!"

Bugs decided to impress Porky

"I Think I'll Hang Around."

with his knowledge of the gold fields, so he said grandly, "The old boy prob'ly latched onto the stuff up in the Clambake!"

Porky was unimpressed. "You mean the Klondike!"

"Well, wherever it was, he's got it, and that's the important thing!"

At that moment somebody in the crowd shouted, "Here he comes!"

"I hope he hasn't run out of gold by the time he rolls by us," Bugs said.

"Naw!" was Porky's confident

"Here He Comes!"

reply. "He's got plenty!"

Both Bugs's and Porky's eyes widened as they watched the approaching car and the bulky figure standing up in the backseat. The surging mob ebbed and flowed away from the car, and the tinkle of coins dropping on the streets could be heard for some distance, along with shouts of "I got mine!" and "Throw some more, Frosty Fred!"

As the car drew nearer, they saw that it was a long, shiny blue car driven by a haughty, uniformed

Scattering Gold Pieces

chauffeur. It moved slowly through
the cheering crowds that lined both
sides of the street. On the car was
a sign: *Frosty Fred, the Klondike
Kid.* And then they saw Frosty
Fred himself.

His round, ruddy face was beaming, and the long white beard
fringing it waved and rippled in
the breeze as he smiled and
acknowledged the cheers of the
crowd. Every few moments he
dipped one hand into a large bag
he held and scattered gold pieces
far and wide on either side of the

Enjoying His Work

car. The people pushed and fought with each other, struggling to grab as many of the coins as possible. Porky and Bugs found themselves pushed, shoved, grabbed at, climbed over, and trampled upon by the mob.

"This thing's a riot!" grunted Bugs as he dodged between threshing arms and legs. "But if there's any gold around to latch onto, Bugsy's going to get his!"

Roly-poly Porky was too busy trying to keep out of the way to talk.

A Mad Rush

"Go get it, boys! Har! Har!" rumbled Frosty Fred as he stood aloof, watching the mob surging back and forth in what amounted to a free-for-all. When the action slowed a little, he would dip into his bag again and start new activity by showering more coins.

As the car and the disorderly mob moved on, a badly buffeted and banged-up Porky and Bugs were left in its wake. Sprawled in the street, Porky nursed his aching head.

"Any luck, Bugs?" he asked.

Sprawled in the Wake of the Crowd

Bugs held up two of the shiny gold coins, one clutched tightly in each hand.

"Yep! Got two of them! See? Any time there's a scramble for a fast buck, here's one bunny that's always in there—scrambling!"

Porky's face fell. He dropped his chin into his hands and tried hard to keep back tears of disappointment. "Shucks!" he faltered. "I didn't get any gold pieces."

Bugs looked at his sad pal and then bared his big front teeth in a wide, jovial grin. He became

"I Got Two of Them!"

Mr. Bighearted Bunny himself.

"Here!" he said grandly, handing one of the gold pieces to Porky. "Take one, doc! As you know, my magnetic personal charm is topped only by my great generosity!"

Porky's chubby face was wreathed in smiles as he looked at the shining coin. "Gee! Thanks, Bugs!" he said.

But Bugs was looking down the street after the mob following Frosty Fred's car. "Boy," he said wonderingly, "that old gent is really doing some high-class stuff!"

Generous Bugs

Porky was satisfied at having one of the gold coins, but Bugs, full of big ideas, was already picturing himself in Frosty Fred's place, tossing gold to his admirers. It was typical of the two pals.

With a dreamy, slap-happy expression on his fuzzy face, Bugs put his hands behind his head and leaned back against the curb. "I'd sure like to zip along in a snazzy car like that and toss gold coins to the admiring peasants whenever I got the urge!"

"You'd have to be as rich as

Bugs Daydreams

Frosty Fred to do that!" Porky pointed out to the dreamy Bugs. "That kind of dough doesn't grow on trees!"

Bugs pulled himself up to a sitting position and scowled. "Yeah," he agreed, "that puts a small bug in the ointment!"

Porky didn't have any such big ideas and was more interested in the immediate prospect of spending money he had in his pocket. "Let's go get a big ice-cream soda!" he suggested.

Bugs looked at Porky Pig with

A Major Problem

disgust. "I got bigger things on my mind than slopping up ice-cream sodas," he said, shaking a finger at Porky as they walked along. "I have to figure out a way to latch onto the kind of dough Frosty Fred tosses around. There's no reason why we can't be as rich as that guy is!"

"But he probably hunted for years up in Alaska before he found all that gold!" Porky complained.

"So what?" Bugs asked. "He doesn't look so bright—that's prob'ly why it took him so long!"

Bugs Has a Solution

The bunny tapped his swelling chest confidently. "With *my* super-brain hitting on all six, we could locate a load of the shiny yellow stuff in a matter of minutes and be richer than Crocus!"

"You mean Croesus," Porky corrected him patiently. "But how are we going to do it?"

Bugs was becoming more excited by the minute as he warmed to his subject. "Why, that's easy!" he proclaimed. "We could whip up to Alaska, dig us some gold, and be set for life! It's all lying right

Bugs Explains His Plan

under the snow! It shouldn't be any job at all to dig it up!"

Porky shook his head, puzzled. "That all sounds swell, but how'll we know where to dig? That's the real secret of finding gold—knowing where to start digging!" he explained.

Bugs looked at Porky as though it were hard for him to understand how anyone could be so stupid. "I tell you, I've got a plan," he said impatiently. "We take a run out to Frosty Fred's dump, have a chat with the old geezer, and he tells us

"How Do We Find the Gold?"

where to go to look for the gold!"

Porky mulled this over the rest of the way home, and, after Bugs had gotten out his little roadster for the run to Frosty Fred's, the chubby little pig was ready with another question.

"But if Frosty Fred knows where the gold is," he persisted, "won't he want to keep it a secret from everybody?"

Bugs shifted gears and stepped on the gas. "Why should he want to keep it a secret?" he countered as they shot away from the curb.

On to Frosty Fred's!

"He's got all he needs or wants, hasn't he? Therefore, he should be willing to share the wealth!"

As usual, Porky allowed himself to be convinced against his better judgment, and they were soon on the highway leading to Frosty Fred's luxurious home.

As they drove up to the beautiful mansion, Bugs pointed to it and said, "Boy, look at that shack! When we get back from the Klondike, loaded with gold, we'll have us an igloo like that!"

Porky had caught some of his

A Fast Ride

friend's enthusiasm by this time, and his eyes sparkled as he looked at the place. Bugs put on the brakes, and the little roadster skidded to a stop before the front door. Without a moment's hesitation, the two bounded out of the car.

"Let's get going and get the dope on the gold," said Bugs. "The sooner we find out where this place is, the sooner we get back to enjoy the fruits of our labors!"

As Bugs instructed, Porky reached up to ring the bell, and they heard its tones echo through

They Skidded to a Stop

the house. In a few moments they heard footsteps on the other side of the door, and then it was opened by a ramrod-stiff butler, who glared down at them from under bushy black eyebrows.

"Yes?" he asked coldly.

Bugs matched the butler's glare with one of his own, and said, "Two jolly lads to see Mr. Fred about some gold! Step aside whilst we go in and have words with the master!"

Bugs's brash speech had no effect whatsoever upon the stiff-backed

A Cool Reception

butler. He continued to glare coldly
as he took two steps backward and
started to close the door.

Bugs was quicker than the butler, though, and put his full weight
against the door.

"Mr. Fred's through giving away
gold for today!" the butler said,
trying to close the door.

"Hold it, doc!" Bugs puffed,
keeping his weight against the
door. "We don't want him to give
us any gold! We just want him to
cut us in on where it is!"

When he heard this, the butler's

"Hold It, Doc!"

manner changed completely. He bowed low and opened the door wide. He gave Bugs and Porky an oily smile and said, "Oh, that's different! He's always glad to tell his visitors that!"

Porky was skeptical of this sudden change in the butler's manner, but Bugs figured it was his overpowering personality that had won the butler over. He turned confidently to Porky. "See? I told you he'd be glad to share his secret!"

As they followed the butler down a long, wide hall, Bugs and Porky

A Change of Heart

rubbernecked like a couple of tour-
ists visiting the home of a Holly-
wood movie queen.

"Some dump, hey, Pork?" Bugs
commented, and Porky nodded his
head enthusiastically. He was too
fascinated by it all to speak.

The butler led them into a richly
furnished room at the end of the
hall. Frosty Fred, his white beard
making him look like Santa Claus,
was sitting in a big, comfortable
chair.

Bugs, brash as usual, extended
a hand and said, "Greetings,

Frosty Fred, the Gold King

Frosty! I'm Bugs Bunny, and this is my pal, Porky Pig! We're here to see you about some dope on how to latch onto some gold like that stuff you tossed around today!"

"Pull up a snowball—er—I mean, a chair, and squat, boys!" Frosty Fred grinned.

When they were seated, Bugs launched right into the purpose of their visit.

"What we want to see you about 'specially, Frosty, is where you go in Alaska to latch onto the yellow goodies!" Bugs said.

"Pull Up a Chair, Boys."

The old prospector laughed heartily at the bunny's eagerness. "Oh, ho!" he chuckled. "Want to know where the gold is, eh?"

He stroked his beard, and his blue eyes twinkled. "Well," he continued, "I'm retired, boys, so I'll be glad to show you where I got mine!"

Bugs and Porky leaned forward eagerly. "That'd be more than peachy, doc! Where *did* you get it?" Bugs asked.

"Yeah, where?" asked Porky.

Frosty Fred reached over and

Fred's Eyes Twinkled

rang for the butler. "I tell you, boys, it's a little difficult to show you where the gold is without a map. I'll have Jeeves haul one out, and then I'll mark the place so you won't make any mistakes. Alaska's a mighty big place, and mighty cold, too. You might dig around up there for years like I did, without finding anything, if you don't know where to go."

Smiling his oily smile, the butler brought a rolled-up map to Frosty Fred, while the gold seekers sat by, watching impatiently.

The Butler Brought a Map

As the butler handed him the map, Frosty Fred turned to the excited Bugs and Porky, saying, "Now, boys, I'll show you where the gold is, but there's *one little condition* you must agree to!"

Speaking together, Porky and Bugs faltered, "Condition?"

Noting their disappointment, Frosty Fred said in his bluff way, "Now, now, boys, it isn't as bad as that! After all, I'm giving you all the dope on how to find the gold, right? You boys ought to be willing to do a little favor for old Frosty!

"There's One Little Condition."

All I'm asking is a measly little old
one-third of all the ore you find up
there. That's not so bad, is it?
You'll have all the rest!"

Bugs dismissed the "condition"
with an airy wave of his hand. "A
mere nothing, doc," he said. "We'll
be happy to split the gold three
ways!"

Porky and Bugs watched impatiently as Frosty Fred slowly un-
furled the map. He picked up a
pencil, and it was lost in his beard
for a second as he wet the tip with
his tongue.

"A Mere Nothing, Doc."

Then he began tracing on the map with the pencil, mumbling to himself. Finally he stopped the pencil and made a mark.

"Where I'm pointing is just about the location of the mother lode!" he said.

Bugs looked at Porky, saw his blank expression, and then looked at Frosty Fred, scratching his head in bewilderment. "I don't get it, Frosty," Bugs said. "Mamma load? What's that?"

The old prospector's white beard waggled up and down as he laughed

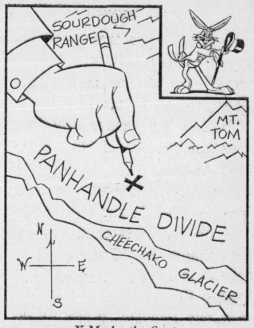

X Marks the Spot

heartily. "Har! Har! You boys are sure tenderfeet! The mother lode is the main source of the gold! That's where most of it is!"

"Well, if you don't ask, you don't find out anything!" Bugs replied. Then he took the map, spread it on the floor, and pored over it. Porky watched, too. "That mother lode is what we want a *load of!*" Bugs said happily.

While Bugs and Porky studied the map, Frosty Fred left the room for a few minutes. When he returned, he handed Bugs a paper

Bugs and Porky Study the Map

with a list of items on it.

"Since you boys aren't very experienced in the prospecting business, I made up a list of the things you'll need for gold digging! You'd better buy everything here, 'cause you won't find the stuff up in the Klondike!"

Bugs grabbed the list, saying, "Much obliged to you, doc! We're off now, and we'll bring you back your third of what we discover."

As they left the prospector's mansion, Bugs clutched the map tightly. The old man stood in the

A List of Things to Buy

door, chuckling. He waved good-bye and wished them luck.

"Don't think we don't depreciate all you've done for us, 'cause we do!" Bugs called back over his shoulder.

"You bet!" Porky added. For one who had at first been so luke-warm to the gold-hunting idea, Porky was showing the same excitement that had taken hold of Bugs.

"Well," said Bugs, getting into the roadster, "we got all the dope, and we're practic'ly loaded down

"Good Luck, Boys!"

with gold right now!"

Porky sat in the car, beaming. "Boy, this is wonderful!"

If the enthusiastic gold hunters hadn't been so intent on their good fortune, they might have noticed that Frosty Fred and his oily butler were watching them with a great deal of interest from a window of the mansion.

"There go two more suckers, Frosty," said the butler.

Frosty Fred's eyes glinted coldly as he replied. "Yep! We've got us a sweet little racket, Red! We

"There Go Two More Suckers!"

can't fail. No matter what happens,
we always stand a chance of cash-
ing in on big dough!"

Red pointed in the direction Bugs
and Porky had gone. "Where'd you
send those two?"

"Har! Har! It really doesn't
make much difference! I send each
batch of suckers to a different spot
in Alaska, and we share in what-
ever they find! Some of them are
sure to find gold!"

Red watched admiringly as the
old rascal put a pin into a certain
spot a large wall map of Alaska.

Fred's "Treasure" Map

"I'd better stick a pin into the map at about the spot I sent those last two," he said. "I wouldn't want to get any of our suckers mixed up. We've got quite a gang up there hunting gold for us!"

Frosty Fred was feeling pretty pleased with himself. "All it costs us is a few gold pieces tossed in the street once a year, and the suckers flock to us like crazy. It's the easiest and safest caper I ever thought of!"

"It's a good racket, all right," Red agreed. "But sometimes the whole thing gets on my nerves,

Adding Another Pin

because some of those suckers we
send up there *don't ever come back
from up there!*"

Frosty Fred rolled his eyes upward and assumed a saintly expression.

"Ah, yes, how true!" he said.
"But then—that's life!"

"We'll Hope They Come Back."

CHAPTER 2

PORKY'S SNEEZE

Bugs and Porky worked hard buying the cold-weather equipment Frosty Fred had listed for them— using Porky's money. When they had it all together, it made quite a pile, and while Porky checked to see if they had everything, Bugs said, "Well, we got the stuff; now we need a way to get to Alaska!

Checking Equipment

I've got it! Let's fly!"

"Fly? How?" asked Porky, puzzled.

"In our own plane—how else?" Bugs retorted. "We still have enough of *your* dough to buy a little plane! G'wan, scare one up whilst I study the map Frosty Fred gave us!"

Porky not only found a plane, but he also had the foresight to have skis added to the regular landing ear in order to land on snow and in Alaska. When they got the e loaded with all their gear, it

Almost Ready to Go

was so heavy that Porky, who was piloting, had a hard time getting it off the ground. Finally he got the plane started upward, but they both got a good scare as the plane's fuselage clipped the trees at one end of the airport before they were safely in the air.

When they had recovered from their fright, Bugs yelled to Porky, "Aim her north, doc, and don't spare the icicles!"

"Roger!" Porky said, smiling. "Klondike gold fields, next stop! Hang on!"

Close Call

After several hours of steady flying, both noticed that it was getting much colder. Bugs put on his fur jacket, and then he took over the controls while Porky did the same.

When Porky took the stick again, Bugs got out the map to try to find out where they were.

"Aren't we just about there?" Porky asked, his snout red with cold and a worried look in his eyes.

"Well, we should be reaching our destitution pretty pronto!" Bugs answered, wiggling his ears and

A Worried Porky

looking intently at the map.

In a few minutes Porky jabbed Bugs with his elbow and pointed to the gas gauge. "We'd better be getting where we're going," he yelled over the noise of the motor, "because we're almost out of gas! Look!"

Bugs's eyes popped as he saw the needle wavering toward the "empty" line on the gauge.

"Yi-ipe! It is getting a mite lowly, isn't it?" he said. He took another quick look at the map and then added sadly, "To be brutally

Bugs's Eyes Popped

frank, doc, I'm not exactly sure
where we are—except that it's
Alaska!" At that remark, Porky
became so excited that Bugs
couldn't even make out what he
was stuttering about when he
started to talk. Finally Bugs said,
"Don't fret so, doc! When we see
some folks, we'll land and get our
directions!"

Porky stuttered in reply, "Well,
w-w-we'd better s-s-see some folks,
because we're landing right now!"

The plane banked sharply as the
motor sputtered on the last drop

"Don't Fret So, Doc!"

of gas. They lost altitude rapidly, and Bugs lost all his customary cockiness.

"Take it easy, doc," he implored Porky. "Remember we got a whole box of dynamite in this thing!"

Porky was too busy trying to make a landing, without breaking both their necks, to pay any attention. He tried desperately to hold the plane steady as it wavered down, pulled steadily earthward by its heavy load. Spying a level spot between the towering ice cliffs, he maneuvered the plane onto it, and

Emergency Landing

both braced themselves for the ex-
pected shock. It turned out to be
a fairly gentle one, and the plane
nosed over into a snow bank with
a thump.

Safely on the ground, Bugs became his own brash self again. He
started to open the door of the
plane, but the icy blasts outside
made it a difficult job.

"C'mon, Porky!" he said. "Let's
get out of here and start digging
up the yellow stuff! There's no time
like the present!"

Bugs was so excited he had a

Safe on the Ground

hard time getting on the snowshoes Porky insisted they wear. When they got outside the plane, he jumped up and down, pointing to the hard-packed snow and ice.

"There might be gold right here under our tootsies!" he exclaimed exultantly.

Porky scowled at him. "Mebbe so, b-b-but let's f-find shelter before we f-freeze."·

Bugs did a great job of unloading all their heavy equipment—right onto Porky's aching back. As he put the box of dynamite on top of the

"Maybe There's Gold Right Here!"

load, he warned Porky about it.

"Be careful of this stuff, doc! It isn't firecrackers, you know!"

Staggering under the heavy load, Porky managed to grunt, "Okay!" They started off toward a towering, frosty cliff in an effort to gain some protection from the biting wind. Carrying nothing, Bugs moved along fast on his snowshoes, while Porky struggled behind.

Finally Bugs motioned impatiently. "C'mon, doc!" he said. "Do you want to freeze in your tracks?"

Porky Struggled Behind

"I'm so loaded down that I'm about to drop in them!" Porky retorted.

As they stopped for Porky to get his breath, he straightened suddenly under his heavy load, and his face screwed up in a grimace.

"Hey! What's the matter?" Bugs asked.

"I think I'm going to sneeze!" He no sooner got the words out when the prodigious *a-achoo!* followed and echoed from the surrounding cliffs.

Suddenly the sound of Porky's

A-CHOO!

sneeze was drowned out by a mighty 'rumble that merged into a tremendous roar. The two gold hunters looked at each other, terrified, and then turned their eyes upward. They saw a mighty mass of snow and ice, loosened from the cliff, tumbling toward them.

"Run for your life, doc!" Bugs shouted, but his words were wasted, for Porky was already moving fast considering the load on his back. He was just a few steps behind Bugs and out of danger when the ice mass hit bottom with a

Avalanche!

terrific *kerwhomp!*

They watched while the snow
and ice settled and the noise sub-
sided. Then Bugs said, "Now what
do you s'pose made that baby
relapse like that?"

"I read somewhere that sometimes a little sound like a whistle
or a sneeze will make an ice wall
crumble!" Porky explained.

"It's amazing!" Bugs exclaimed,
and then he pointed excitedly as his
eyes fell on an opening in the ice
wall. "Hey! Look at the big hole,
Porky! It looks like it might be a

"Hey! Look at the Big Hole!"

tunnel or something!"

As they moved closer for a better look, they saw what appeared to be a long passageway lined with pillars made of a hard, yellow, shiny metal.

"What do you s'pose it is?" Porky asked, looking at Bugs and scratching his head, puzzled.

"I dunno," Bugs answered, equally puzzled, "but there's only one way to find out. Let's mosey on in!"

As they walked down the silent passage, both looked at the curious

Mysterious Pillars

carvings on the metal pillars. The more Porky looked at the pillars, the more he became convinced that they were made of solid gold. He was almost afraid to mention it to Bugs, but finally he said, "Bugs! Do you s'pose these pillars are made of *gold?*"

Bugs put his hands on one of the pillars and inspected it closely. "There's only one way to find out," he announced. "The tooth test!"

Porky watched as Bugs bent forward quickly and clamped his teeth on a section of the pillar.

The "Tooth Test"

Bugs threw his arms around the pillar as far as they would go and hugged it. "Brace yerself, doc!" he shouted happily. "Happy days have just arrived! It *is* gold!"

Bugs's joy was cut short, however, as Porky nervously poked him in the back and said, "B-Bugs! Look! Over there!" He pointed.

Bugs looked and gulped. His knees began shaking uncontrollably. What he saw was a very large individual, dressed in a strange-looking uniform, approaching up the passage, followed by two others

A Stranger Approached

equally as big. They looked like guards or sentries.

"Who do you suppose they are?" Porky whispered.

"I dunno, doc—but they don't look like any welcoming committee to me!" Bugs faltered in a quavering voice as the light from the strangers' torches fell full on them.

Then the leader spotted the two shivering intruders and came forward, glaring at them. He held his torch high, so he could see them better, and then addressed Bugs. His deep voice echoed from the

The Leader Glared at Them

walls of the passage.

"Who are you who enter the kingdom of Radiom?" he asked. "And how did you find our secret entrance from the outside world?"

Bugs decided to try to bluff it through, so he put on a bold front and said, "Well, doc, you might say we sneezed our way in!"

"What's this? Sneezed?"

Bugs then quickly explained how Porky's sneeze had caused the snowslide, revealing the entrance to the passage. "And now," he finished, "I'm going to fling a couple

"We Sneezed Our Way In!"

of well-chosen questions at you
guys! What is this dump, anyway?"

Amused by Bugs's brashness, the
leader of the uniformed men smiled
and motioned for Bugs and Porky
to follow him and his aides.

"Come with us, strangers, and
we'll show you our city!"

Bugs and Porky decided it would
be a good idea to go along.

"Come With Us."

CHAPTER 3

THE KINGDOM OF RADIOM

As they walked along the passage, their guide identified himself as Blimpo, captain of the King's Guards, and explained how the kingdom of Radiom had thrived beneath the ice and snow for thousands of years.

"But doesn't it get awful cold and dark down in this bloated mole

"I'm Blimpo."

hole?" Bugs asked curiously.

"No!" answered Blimpo. "Long ago we discovered the basic secret of heat and light—radium!"

Suddenly, after walking along the passage for several minutes, they came to its end and saw spread out before them a glistening city of majestic towers and bridges.

The shock of seeing the glittering city left Bugs and Porky speechless for a moment. When he found his tongue, Bugs said, "Jeepers! It looks like all the buildings are made out of—"

The Kingdom of Radiom

"Gold!" Porky finished.

"Of course!" Blimpo put in. "We have more gold than anything else! We use it for almost everything!"

Bugs and Porky were so busy inspecting the gold sidewalks and curbstones that they failed to notice they were approaching a building constructed of a metal which looked drab and dull compared to the glittering gold on all sides.

"We are coming to the king's palace!" Blimpo announced.

"Hey! How come it isn't made out of shiny gold like the other

The King's Palace

joints?" Bugs asked.

"Because it's made of lead—our most valuable metal," Blimpo explained patiently. "Only lead is fitting for a king's palace and treasure!"

Uniformed guards and lackeys were stationed all over the palace, and, motioning to one of them, Blimpo said, "Announce us to the king!"

Even Bugs, who ordinarily had little respect for anybody or anything, was impressed by the fact that they were going to meet the

"Announce Us to the King!"

king of this fabulous land.

"How come you are going to introduce us to the king?" he asked.

"Because you're the first outsiders we've seen in more than five hundred years!"

Bugs had little chance to mull over this information, for they were approaching the king's throne, and, as Bugs looked up, he saw that the monarch was a handsome youth who appeared to be still in his teens. The king was intently reading a scroll and did not notice them immediately.

A Youthful King

"He looks awfully young to be the big wheel around here!" Bugs whispered to Blimpo.

"He *is* young!" Blimpo answered. "He's only nine hundred years old!"

All this was too much for Bugs, and Porky, too. Bugs could hardly keep quiet until they had been presented to the king.

Then he said, "I hope I'm not talking out of turn, Your Honor, but before we were introduced, your crony, here, said you were nine hundred years old. You look like a

An Amazing Discovery

kid! What's the gag?"

The king smiled. "I *am* nine hundred years old! We've discovered that radium, as well as being the source of our heat and light, also holds the secret of long life."

Bugs had more questions he would have liked to ask, but the king kept Bugs and Porky so busy answering *his* questions about the outside world that the bunny's went unasked.

Suddenly, in the middle of their discussion, they heard a loud noise behind them, and the king's eyes

The King Questioned Bugs and Porky

widened in fright as he looked up.

"The men from Polaris!" he cried, as two fur-covered figures approached, brandishing strange-looking weapons.

"They've got their ice guns!" Blimpo yelled.

At that moment, one of the men pointed his ice gun at the young king and fired. There was a blast of cold air, and the young king became instantly rigid, frozen like a block of ice.

As two men from Polaris carried off the king, another pointed

Strange Men and Weapons

his gun at Bugs and said, "I'll freeze this fuzzy one and all the others!"

The last thing Bugs remembered before freezing up was seeing the king being borne off on the shoulders of the invaders.

Frozen Solid

CHAPTER 4

THROUGH THE WALL

It was several hours before the warm air of Radiom thawed Bugs, Porky, and Blimpo so that they could move freely.

Bugs began threshing his arms around to start his blood circulating again. He tried to find out from Blimpo what had happened. That roly-poly individual, however,

Thawing Out

seemed able only to moan over and over, "This is terrible! Oh, this is terrible!"

Finally Bugs, continuing to beat himself with his arms, said, "C'mon, doc, pull yourself together! Where's the king?"

Tears rolled down Blimpo's pudgy nose as he whimpered and blubbered.

"Those were the men from Polaris," he sniffled. "That's another underground kingdom nearby, but it's very primitive and warlike. They've been trying to

Tears Rolled Down His Nose

capture our king for thousands of years!"

"Well, this is one time they sure receded!" Bugs admitted. "But this isn't any time to cry over spilt ice water! Where's the way to this Polaris dump, and what's the procedure for getting the king back?"

For an answer, Blimpo opened his mouth wider and wailed louder. "They won't give him back!" he sobbed. "He's gone for good—and, what's worse, only the king knows the secret of the power of radium. We'll have no heat or light!"

"Where's This Polaris Dump?"

Bugs was becoming more annoyed with Blimpo by the second for his continued wailing and his failure to make any effort to rescue the king.

Shouting, to make himself heard over Blimpo's wails, Bugs said, "Well, don't just stand around blubbering! Round up your army and make a nonsociable call on those bums!"

Blimpo was so surprised at this remark that he stopped crying. "But we have no army and only simple weapons!" he whimpered.

Bugs Became Angry

"How do you like that?" Bugs asked nobody in particular. "These jerks put the king in a deep freeze and cart him off, and this outfit hasn't even got a defroster!"

"If there were only some way to rescue our king!" Blimpo moaned. "But it's hopeless!"

"Nothing is hopeless, doc! Where is this Polaris burg?" asked Bugs.

"Past our city and through the endless cavern!" Blimpo said mournfully. "We have a wall there to keep the Polaris men out, but somehow they got through!"

Bugs Asks Directions

Bugs brightened. "Well, if they came through the wall *this* way, we can go through the *other* way!"

Blimpo turned around quickly, his eyes wide with fright. "'We'? You don't mean—"

"Sure!" Bugs said expansively. "Me and Porky'll try to get your king back for you! You're a bunch of nice guys, and we'd hate to see you turn into a flock of icebergs!"

Porky didn't share Bugs's enthusiasm. "Hey! Wait a minute! I didn't say anything about—" he started.

"We'll Get Your King Back!"

"Quiet!" Bugs cut him off. "Bring some of our junk! We may need it!"

Porky went off, mumbling to himself, to get the equipment, and in a few minutes they were following Blimpo to the entrance of the endless cavern. After they had trudged some distance, Blimpo stopped and pointed down a long passage.

"There's the cavern! Go straight ahead, and good luck!"

There was no sound except that of their hesitant footsteps as Bugs

Off to the Rescue

and Porky walked along the rocky floor of the cavern. Finally they came to the place Blimpo had told them about—the walled-up spot where the Polaris men had broken through. There was a big jagged hole in the wall.

Pointing, Bugs said, "Well, there's the wall they ejected to keep those bums out of Radiom!"

Porky looked around nervously. "And there's where they dug through it, too! I wonder if any of them are hanging around here," he said anxiously.

There Was a Hole in the Wall!

After telling Porky that the Polaris men were probably holding a celebration to honor the king-snatching, Bugs stepped through the hole in the wall and reached back to get the bundle of equipment from Porky.

They proceeded slowly on the Polaris side of the passage.

"It's sure dark in here!" said Porky.

"You aren't just gnashing your teeth, doc!" Bugs returned. "But I think I spy some light up yonder! C'mon, let's go!"

Entering the Land of Polaris

As they approached it, the spot
of light became bigger, and soon
they could tell it was the end of the
passage. Slowly the two adventurers crawled out of the passage and
to the edge of an overhanging cliff.
Below them was a group of circular
huts, and they could make out
figures dancing around a huge fire.

After they had watched the
scene a few minutes in silence,
Porky asked, "Where do you s'pose
they've got the king?"

Bugs pointed at a hut outside
which two fierce-looking Polaris

They Watched From the Cliff

men stood guard. "Probably in that joint over there! That's what the guards are for!"

Drops of nervous perspiration stood out on Porky's brow despite the cold. Bugs concentrated heavily. "We've got to get him out of there before they do him some dirt!" Bugs said.

"Don't you think we should scout around some first?" Porky asked nervously.

Bugs began crawling determinedly toward the hut. "Nope! We'd best do it now whilst they're

"The King's in That Hut!"

blowing their tops singing and dancing, doc!"

Near the hut Bugs stopped and whispered for Porky to give him a couple of sticks of dynamite and some matches.

"What are you going to do with them?" Porky asked.

Bugs grinned. "Nothing, *now!* But later we'll scare the fur off them with it! Yessir, they ought to get a real bang out of this dynamite!"

Porky chewed his nails and watched every move Bugs made.

Inching Toward Danger

Bugs finally disappeared from his sight and was gone several minutes. Suddenly Bugs reappeared, running as fast as he could. He lurched into Porky.

"Stand back, doc, and await results!" he panted. "They ought to come pretty quick—and be red hot!"

Bugs had hardly spoken the words when his prophecy came true. There were shouts of mingled rage and pain, and Porky could see the guards jumping up and down, each one holding one of his feet.

Red-Hot Hotfoot

Answering Porky's questioning
look, Bugs chortled, "I slipped them
a hotfoot! Let's go get the king!"

The guards' confusion left the
entrance to the hut unguarded, and
both Bugs and Porky were able to
slip inside. They found the king,
frozen rigid.

"He's still a human ice cube!"
Bugs whispered. "Help me pick
him up!"

Struggling with their heavy
burden, they were able to get him
outside and start toward the entrance to the endless cavern, still

A Human Ice Cube

unobserved by the guards.

Looking back over his shoulder,
Bugs said, "They're so busy figger-
ing out what toasted their tootsies
that they've forgotten all about the
king."

"I hope they *keep* forgetting!"
panted Porky.

But that was too much to hope.
In a few moments they heard the
shout from below: "The king is
gone!"

Porky pulled up short as Bugs
ordered him to drop the king. Then
Bugs reached into his parka and

Making Their Escape

brought out the dynamite sticks he had been saving. He lit the fuse and went into his best pitching windup.

"I'll toss them a curve that they won't forget!" Bugs said, gritting his teeth.

"Stop talking and throw!"

Bugs tossed with a full follow-through. The flaming fuse made a bright arc as it moved through the semidarkness of the cavern entrance. Seconds later there were two terrific explosions. *Blam! Blam!* The blasts echoed from the

Playing With Dynamite

rocky, ice-covered walls.

Picking up the rigid king, Bugs and Porky sped again toward the hole in the wall which would get them back into Radiom. Panting and out of breath, they got there safely, but they could hear the pounding steps of the Polaris men not far behind.

They pushed the king through the hole first, and, as they were accomplishing this task, Porky urged Bugs to hurl some more dynamite to stop the advancing Polaris men.

Safety Just Ahead

"No time now! Let's get through the hole first!"

With the king through the hole, Bugs and Porky were able to move faster. "Here I go!" Bugs said, diving through the hole.

"Hurry up!" Porky urged desperately. "These guys with their ice guns are getting close enough to put me in another deep freeze! Hurry!"

The chubby Porky got his head and shoulders through the hole, but for several agonizing moments it seemed very likely that the rest of

"Hurry Up, Bugs!"

him wasn't going to make it.

"Deflate yourself!" Bugs grunted, struggling with one of Porky's
arms.

"I'm making myself as skinny as
I can! Pull hard!" Porky panted.

Bugs dug in his heels, gritted his
teeth, and heaved mightily. Something gave, and Porky came hur-
tling through the hole.

"Wow! That was a closie!
Where's the box of dynamite?"

"It's on the other side!" Porky
mourned. "I couldn't get through
the hole with it on!" Porky pointed

A Tight Fit

to the size of the hole to emphasize his point.

Bugs put his hands on his hips and scowled. He wasn't angry at Porky, but he was trying to figure out a way to explode the dynamite without going through the hole again.

"This is what is known as a predicament, doc," he announced. "It calls for some special work from my super brain—and quick!"

Bugs cocked an ear in the direction of the hole. "*Yipe!* Those Polaris jerks are practically at the

"This Is a Predicament, Doc."

other side of the hole!"

Porky was pessimistic. "They
will get us sure with those ice
guns!"

Suddenly Bugs grinned. He
reached inside his parka and
brought out a box of matches.

"No, they won't!" he said. "Not
if we have any luck—and I don't
think *all* of old Bugsy's has run out
yet!"

He opened the matchbox, took
out a match, lit it, and jammed it,
burning, back among the others
inside the box.

"Our Luck Hasn't Run Out Yet!"

"Hey!" Porky protested. "You're lighting all of our matches at once!"

Bugs held the box gingerly as he watched the rest of the matches inside burst into flame.

"You aren't giving me any news flash, doc!" he said to Porky, then turned quickly and thrust the flaming box of matches at the hole in the wall. "Cross your fingers, Porky! If only *one* of those matches hits the dynamite, we're okay!"

The next few seconds seemed like hours. The pounding footsteps

Desperation Toss

of the vicious men from Polaris
sounded closer and closer. The
z-zap! z-zap! of the ice guns grew
ominously louder.

"I guess we're licked," Porky
said mournfully. "I can feel ice
forming on me already!"

His last words were drowned by
an earsplitting explosion, followed
by the crash of falling rock. The
concussion flung both Porky and
Bugs up against the wall of the
cavern and then dropped them to
the ground.

It all happened so quickly that

An Earsplitting Explosion

Bugs wasn't sure whether the dynamite had exploded or whether he had been subjected to the quick-freeze treatment by the ice guns of the men from Polaris. His head was still whirling from the impact, but he opened an eye anyway. The first thing he saw was a huge pile of earth and stone.

"Well, *something* happened, anyway!" he muttered, turning to Porky, who was moving feebly and making strange noises.

"Whee-oo!" Porky exhaled. "What happened?"

Stunned Companions

"You may uncross your fingers, doc!" Bugs exulted. He pointed to the landslide of earth and rock effectively blocking the passage. "That tunnel is really clamped shut for good! Those hairy apes won't get through *there* again!"

"You boys are certainly right!" another voice chimed in. Bugs and Porky turned quickly and saw the king sitting up and smiling. In all the excitement of the escape from the villains of Polaris, they had forgotten him.

"Well, I see you've defrosted!"

A Defrosted King

Bugs greeted the king. "I guess that blast of dynamite was enough to loosen anything! I'm not even sure I've got my teeth yet!"

The king stood up stiffly and brushed remaining particles of ice from his royal robes. He reached out a hand and patted an embarrassed Porky on the head.

"I'll never know how to thank you boys!" he said seriously. "You've saved Radiom!"

"Aw, shucks!" Porky said, looking at the ground.

Then Bugs turned his head away

"You've Saved Radium!"

coyly and blinked. " 'Twasn't anything much, doc!" he said, but to
himself he figured that rescuing the
king ought to be worth a reward
that would put both Porky and himself on Easy Street.

The smiling king put one arm
around Porky and the other around
Bugs. "No matter how much you
protest," he said, "I'm going to see
that you are rewarded hand-
somely!"

Porky's chubby face creased into
a wide grin, while Bugs's eyes
sparkled with happy anticipation,

"I'll See That You Are Rewarded!"

and his long, floppy ears stood up like a couple of Roman candles.

"Well, as long as you put it that way, doc. . . ." Bugs's voice trailed off as they started down the passage.

"The first thing, however, is to make you two heroes comfortable with fresh, warm clothes!" said the king as they neared the Radiom end of the passage.

"Right, doc!" Bugs agreed. "I might even agree to a slight going-over with soap and water!"

"Me, too!" added Porky.

Back to Radiom

CHAPTER 5

A STRATEGIC SNEEZE

After a hot bath, some food, and a good rest, Porky and Bugs decided it was time to go to see the king.

After they had put on the clothes laid out for them by the royal servants, Porky looked himself over carefully and said, "These clothes are pretty, but they sure

New Outfits

feel awfully funny!"

"They're kind of heavy, aren't they?" Bugs agreed. "But I s'pose up here in the Klondike they need thick stuff. Anyway, I'm for heading to see our pal, the king, and latching onto the handsome reward he promised!"

The heavy clothes weighed down Bugs and Porky more than ever as they walked through the high, vaulted halls toward the king's throne room.

"I figure about a ton or so of gold would be fair pay for our little

Going to See the King

job of rescuing the king, don't
you?" Bugs asked Porky as they
walked along.

"That would be swell!" Porky
agreed, but he was serious as he
went on. "Our gold won't do us
much good, though, if we haven't
got a way to get it home!"

"Oh, I figure we can borrow
enough gas to get home on!" Bugs
said airily.

"These people never heard of
gasoline!" said Porky.

"Oh, well! Time enough to worry
about that *after* we get the gold!

"Time Enough to Worry Later!"

We'll find some way to get home!"

The king was waiting for them in the throne room, and on a small wagon in front of him was a heavy chest. While the king recounted to the members of his court his heroic rescue by Bugs and Porky, the eyes of the adventurers were on the chest.

"Boy, that baby holds puhlenty of the yellow stuff!" Bugs whispered to Porky.

"You said it! But I'd feel a lot better if we had some way to get it home from here!"

Presenting the Reward

Just then the king finished his speech, concluding, "And now, on behalf of the people of Radiom, I hereby bestow on you this priceless gift!"

Bugs was in no mood for long thank-you speeches. He simply said, "Thanks a trillion, doc! Now we'll be heading home!"

With Porky pushing the wagon while Bugs pulled, they started to leave the throne room, but the king became greatly excited and called them back.

"But you *can't* go!" the king

Homeward Bound—Maybe

said, scowling darkly. His manner had changed completely from the friendliness of a few moments before. "When people enter Radiom, they must stay forever!"

Bugs hesitated only a moment to scowl back at the king. "Don't get me wrong, doc!" he said. "I like you guys swell, but not swell enough to live here! C'mon, Porky!" Complete surprise held everyone in the throne room motionless for a few seconds, but it was long enough for Bugs and Porky to get a head start.

"You Must Stay Forever!"

With Bugs pulling from the front and Porky pushing from behind, they got the wagon rolling and headed for the door, amid a scene of great confusion. The king was yelling to stop them, guards were bumping into each other, and, in the middle of it all, Porky and Bugs scooted along with their wagonload of treasure.

By the time they got to the throne room entrance, one of the guards on duty had recovered enough to try to block the way. Bugs managed to dodge past him,

A Scene of Great Confusion

and Porky, bringing up the rear, handed him a straight-arm that would have done credit to an All-American football player.

"Flee like you've never fleed before!" panted Bugs.

"Just keep going so I don't run over you!" Porky shot back.

They picked up speed down the gold-pillared halls and shot around corners with the same speed that had carried them away from their Polaris pursuers. They found the hole in the ice cliff through which they had entered Radiom and

Flight for Freedom

headed for it. The wagon was heavy, and both were tiring fast as they neared the patch of daylight. Finally they bolted out into the brilliant daylight.

"We're out!" Bugs yelled as they slowed the wagon to a stop.

"Yeah! But they'll pull us right back in! What'll we do?" Porky asked worriedly.

Bugs was his old cocky self as he turned to Porky and said, "It's simple, doc! All you have to do is haul off and let go with a sneeze! That'll bring down a slab of snow

Outside the Tunnel at Last!

and seal them off again!"

"But what if I can't sneeze?" Porky wailed. "I sure don't feel like it right now!"

"But, doc, you *have* to sneeze! It's vital! It's necessary, too! C'mon!"

Whether it was just luck, or whether Bugs's imploring had anything to do with it, will never be known, but at that moment, as if by a signal, Porky's snout wrinkled up. He began taking in short little breaths as he moved his head backward, farther and farther.

"Doc, You HAVE to Sneeze!"

"Ah—ah—ah—" Porky snorted.

"C'mon, Porky! Stop huffing and start sneezing. I can hear those guys coming down the hall, and they don't sound happy!"

There was a horrible moment of indecision as Porky rolled his eyes and gazed agonizingly at Bugs.

Then it came!

"Ah-ah-ah-*choo!*" spluttered Porky, and the sound rumbled among the crannies of the ice cliff. Then came the ominous rumble that both recognized.

"Let's go!" Bugs yelled. He

A Tremendous Sneeze

grabbed Porky and pulled him away just in time. The rumble grew to a roar, and the huge mass of snow threw up a dense curtain of white as it struck bottom, causing a tremendous vibration.

When the mist of snow dust had settled, Bugs pointed happily to the pile of snow and ice which again sealed the entrance to Radiom.

"That was what could be called a strategic sneeze, doc! Those guys are back in cold storage for another five hundred years!"

The more practical Porky was

Sealing the Entrance

not happy. He looked grim as he slumped down on the front of the wagon, and after Bugs looked at him, he, too, realized that things weren't any too rosy.

"What was I grinning about?" he asked. "There're still a couple of minor problems left for us to dissolve!"

"Yeah," said Porky, his chin in his hands. "And the first one is how to get home without being frozen first!"

They decided that they could keep warmer in the plane, which

Things Still Weren't Rosy

was still where they had left it, so they pushed the wagon in that direction. They made another futile search for a can of gasoline that they might have overlooked, but found none.

Bugs brightened some, though, when his eyes fell again on the chest they had brought out of Radiom. "Oh, well," he said, "at least I can take a gander at our gold! I wonder how you get this chest open."

Porky couldn't be comforted by the sight of gold, however, and he looked away toward the distant

Bugs Tries to Open the Chest

horizon, tears welling in his eyes.
Suddenly he blinked the tears away.
He thought his eyes must be playing tricks on him, but he was sure
he saw some objects moving in the
distance.

Porky's yell jerked Bugs away
from his unsuccessful efforts to
open the chest.

"Look!" Porky demanded.

Unmistakable now, as they lum-
bered closer, Bugs and Porky saw
a fleet of army tanks and half-
tracks. For a moment neither could
say anything. Then they both began

Porky Pointed Excitedly

waving their arms and shouting like mad.

"It's the army! It's the army!" Bugs yelled. "We're saved!"

They ran toward the closest vehicle, and, when they were a few feet away, a fur-covered figure poked its head out of the cab and looked curiously at the two figures dressed in the colorful robes which had been given them by the king of Radiom. Even in his furs, the man had the unmistakable stamp of the United States Army on him.

He waved a mittened hand at

The Army to the Rescue!

them and said, "What are you two
doing away up here?"

"I might ask you the same question, doc!" Bugs came back. "But
I'm too happy to see you!"

"We're part of 'Operation
Shiver,'" the soldier said. "We're
testing new army equipment!"

"In that case," Bugs said, "you
must be practic'ly lousy with gas!
How about lending us some for our
plane so we can get out of here and
stop shivering?"

"Sure thing!" The soldier
brought out several large gasoline

Necessary Supplies

cans. "Will that be enough?"

"It sure will—and hooray for the United States Army!" Bugs shouted.

Bugs and Porky put the gas in their plane, hoisted their valuable chest aboard, and were in the air headed for home in record time. Bugs continued his efforts to get the chest open, while Porky acted as pilot. They were nearly to their home airport before Bugs finally managed to open the lock.

It was a tense moment as Bugs struggled to get the heavy lid up.

Headed for Home

As he worked on the heavy lid he squinted his eyes so that the dazzling gold wouldn't be too much for them. Finally the lid was up far enough so that both could see what was inside. Porky stretched over from his place in the cockpit to peer into the chest.

Bugs's wide mouth curved up in a grin and then dropped suddenly as he got a good look at the contents of the chest.

"It's lead!" he screamed.

"*Lead?*" Porky repeated.

"Now I remember!" Bugs said,

"It's Lead!"

after the first shock of disgust and disappointment was gone. "The guy said lead was the most precious stuff they had—"

"So they gave us a box of lead to reward us!" Porky finished for him.

"Well, we carted it this far; we might as well take it all the way!" Bugs grunted. "Maybe we can sell it to a junkman for a few bucks, anyway!"

They were circling the airport now, and Porky nosed the plane down for a landing.

A Disappointed Bugs

"This is sure a disgusting development!" Bugs groaned as the wheels touched the ground.

Porky was more philosophical. "Yeah, but we should've guessed! We should've remembered what the man said!"

As they left the airport, they were two disgusted and strange-looking figures in their Radiom robes.

The long trip in the plane had soiled their clothes, so Porky said, "Let's take these clothes to the cleaners!"

Home at Last

"Yeah! They're all we've got to show for our troubles, of which we've got more'n our share!" Bugs grumbled. "That Frosty Fred sure gave us a bum steer."

At the cleaners' Bugs was still irritable. The man behind the counter took so much time inspecting the Radiom robes carefully that Bugs growled, "Never mind inspecting them, doc! We want them cleaned—and that's all!"

The man looked at Bugs slowly over his glasses. He said, "You'll have to take them to a jeweler!"

"Just Clean Them, Doc!"

"What do you mean?"

"Just this! They're made out of woven gold. They must be worth a fortune!"

Bugs was dazed. "I can't figure it out!" he said.

"It's easy!" Porky said, grinning. "They used gold for everything—so why not for clothes? No wonder the robes felt funny to us. We were a couple of walking bank vaults!"

Their next stop was a jewelry store, where they left the clothes, coming out with a big payment on

Golden Clothes!

what would eventually be a fortune when the jeweler finished appraising the clothes.

Bugs scratched his head and looked at Porky, who was in a complete daze.

"What do you know!" Bugs said slowly. "Here we nearly broke our backs and our necks, too, hauling that chest of lead around, when all the time we were wearing a wad of dough in these dizzy clothes they gave us up there!"

"Things were sure screwy up there, but they're turning out okay

Happy Partners

down here!" Porky pointed out, recovering.

Bugs had become his normal self again. He pointed a finger at Porky and said, "Now that we're in the big dough, we have a couple of things to attend to—and Frosty Fred is both of them!"

They rented the biggest car they could find, complete with liveried chauffeur, and headed for Frosty Fred's mansion. The old rascal and his dishonest butler saw them as they pulled into the drive.

"Here come that dumb bunny

Riding in Comfort

and pig again," said the butler.

"Har! Har!" rumbled Fred. "Looks like they struck it rich, too, and they've got to split with us!"

Porky and Bugs solemnly carried the heavy chest between them up the walk to the house, as the phony prospector and his stooge watched eagerly.

Inside, Frosty Fred and the butler were all smiles, while Bugs and Porky kept straight faces with an effort.

"We're keeping our part of the agreement!" Bugs said seriously.

Visiting Frosty Fred

He motioned to Fred to lift the lid of the chest. "This is your third of the ore we found in Alaska—good old lead!"

Frosty Fred's eyes, which had been glinting with greed, suddenly glazed as he looked at the hunks of lead Porky was removing from the chest.

He let out something which sounded like a cross between a groan and a growl and then simply sputtered in helpless anger.

"*Almost* the end of a perfect day!" Bugs chortled.

Surprise!

"What do you want to do now?" Porky asked, puzzled. "I think everything's just about perfect!" He picked up the chest.

Bugs grabbed one end and pulled the chest and Porky toward the door. "There's a little matter of giving the peasants a gander at two successful gold prospectors! You don't think I went through all that trouble just to come home and bury myself in my hole, do you?"

As they went down the walk from Frosty Fred's mansion, Bugs added, "You know, this place isn't

A Fast Exit

much of a dump at that! Wait'll
you see the shack I put up!"

They got in the backseat of the
car, and Porky leaned back luxu-
riously on the soft cushions.

"Drive down Main Street,
James," he said grandly.

Bugs was busy digging his fists
into the chest of lead pieces, which
he felt sentimental about, having
hauled it around so much.

"Yeah, take it easy, doc!" he
said to the driver. "We said we
wanted to come back from the
Klondike and toss stuff to the

One Last Look

peasants on the curb—and we're
going to do it!"

A curious crowd gathered as
Bugs stood up and began tossing
the lead pieces grandly on each side
of the car. Nobody even bent down
to pick up the lead. "These peasants
aren't even pleasant!" he said.
"But *I'm* having fun!"

Having a Great Time

Other **BIG LITTLE BOOKS**® Available

*With "FLIP-IT" cartoons

WHITMAN® *Classics*

Books for Your Permanent Library

- BLACK BEAUTY
- LITTLE WOMEN
- HEIDI
- HEIDI GROWS UP
- TOM SAWYER
- HUCKLEBERRY FINN
- THE CALL OF THE WILD
- TREASURE ISLAND
- ALICE IN WONDERLAND
- THE WONDERFUL WIZARD OF OZ
- FAMOUS FAIRY TALES
- ALGONQUIN
- TALES OF POE

WHITMAN® *Full-Length Adventures*

Sports Stories

CELLAR TEAM (baseball)

BASKET FEVER (basketball)

PLAYERS' CHOICE (football)

DRAG STRIP DANGER (racing)

Short Story Collections

ADVENTURE CALLING (outdoor stories)

SHUDDERS (ghost stories)

GOLDEN PRIZE (horse stories)

THAT'S OUR CLEO! (cat stories)

WAY OUT (science fiction stories)

LIKE IT IS (stories for girls)

A BATCH OF THE BEST
(stories for girls)